The Perfect Christmas Picture

BY FRAN MANUSHKIN

Illustrated by Karen Ann Weinhaus

An I CAN READ Book

HARPER & ROW, PUBLISHERS

The Perfect Christmas Picture
Text copyright © 1980 by Frances Manushkin
Illustrations copyright © 1980 by Karen Ann Weinhaus
Printed in
the United States of America. For information address
Harper & Row, Publishers, Inc., 10 East 53rd Street,
New York, N.Y. 10022. Published simultaneously in
Canada by Fitzhenry & Whiteside Limited, Toronto.

FIRST EDITION

Library of Congress Cataloging in Publication Data
Manushkin, Fran
    The perfect Christmas picture.

    (An I can read book)
    SUMMARY: Mr. Green tries repeatedly to get the perfect
Christmas picture of his rambunctious family.
    [1. Christmas stories.   2. Family life—Fiction.
3. Photography—Fiction]   I. Weinhaus, Karen Ann.
II. Title.
PZ7.M3195Pe   [E]   79-2678   ER
ISBN 0-06-024068-7   MAU
ISBN 0-06-024069-5 lib. bdg.

7|56

To
Shirley Jacobson,
Sam Manushkin,
Robert Mann,
Richard Mann,
and Sandra Krugman

It was spring.

"Ho!" said Mr. Green.

"What a perfect day

to take a picture of our family

for Christmas."

Mrs. Green laughed.

"Christmas is nine months away.

We have plenty of time."

"I'm not so sure," said Mr. Green.

So he called the children,

Shirley and Sammy,

and

Robert and Richie,

6

and

Frances and Sandy.

They stood in a row

like tulips.

But just as Mr. Green

clicked the camera,

Shirley pinched Sammy,

and Sammy pinched Robert,

who cried.

"Drat!" said Mr. Green.

"That's a terrible picture."

Soon it was summer.

The trees were blooming,

and the birds were chirping.

"Such a splendid day

to take a Christmas picture,"

said Mr. Green.

"Yes it is," agreed Mrs. Green.

Mr. Green called

Shirley and Sammy,

and

Robert and Richie,

14

and

Frances and Sandy.

They stood in a line

like birds on

a telephone wire.

But just as Mr. Green

clicked the camera,

Robert's snake

hissed at Richie's frog,

who plopped into a puddle

and spattered everyone.

17

"Horrible picture!"

yelled Mr. Green.

"But the frog is safe,"

said Mrs. Green.

In midsummer,

the golden sun

gave the children

rich brown tans.

"I think I will try

to take the Christmas picture,"

said Mr. Green.

"Yes," said Mrs. Green,

"let's *try*."

So

Shirley and Sammy,

and

Robert and Richie,

22

and

Frances and Sandy

bunched together

like ducks on a pond.

But just as Mr. Green

clicked the camera,

Frances tripped

on the garden hose

and did a somersault.

"I can do that too!" yelled Sandy,

and she turned three!

"That's an awful picture,"

wailed Mr. Green.

He caught a cold

and went to bed early.

Mrs. Green read him a story.

Autumn came.

The children carved pumpkins

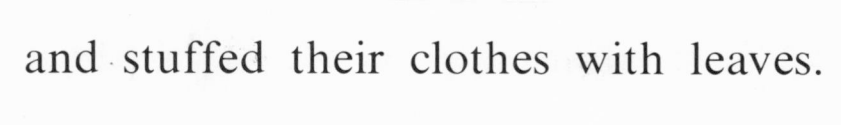

and stuffed their clothes with leaves.

29

"Hey," called Mr. Green.

"Let's take the Christmas picture in this colorful tree."

"Be careful!" said Mrs. Green.

Shirley and Sammy,

and

Robert and Richie,

32

and

Frances and Sandy

held on to the tree

like happy apples.

33

But just as Mr. Green

clicked the camera,

Shirley hiccuped

and bumped into Sammy,

34

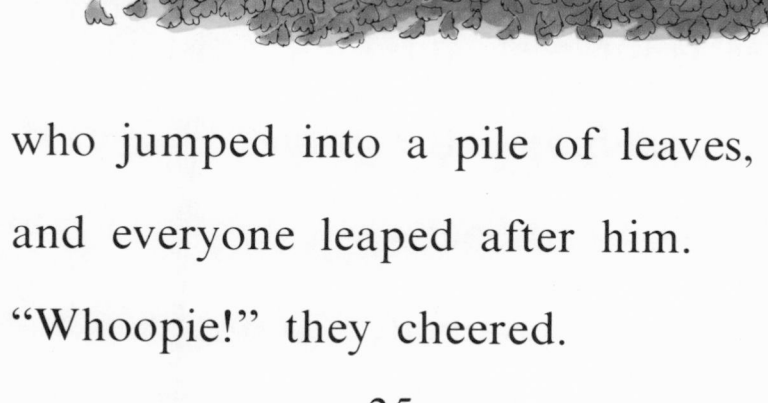

who jumped into a pile of leaves,

and everyone leaped after him.

"Whoopie!" they cheered.

35

Mr. Green stamped his feet

and hid in the garage

biting his nails.

Mrs. Green put Band-Aids on.

The first snow came early,

and the Green family bundled up

for skating and sledding.

"Today," said Mr. Green,

"I'm going to take

the perfect Christmas picture."

"Not again!" said Mrs. Green.

"Nothing can go wrong this time,"

said Mr. Green.

"This time, I am taking

a *moving* picture."

"Poor Daddy," said Shirley.

"We messed up

all of his pictures."

"This is his last chance," said Sammy.

"It has to be perfect," said Robert.

"I know what to do," said Richie.

"This time, we will not move at all.

Then the picture will be fine."

"And Daddy will be happy,"

said Frances.

"And Mother too," said Sandy.

So

Shirley and Sammy,

and

Robert and Richie,

44

and

Frances and Sandy

lined up

and stood

as still as snowmen.

45

"Move!" yelled Mr. Green.

"Skate!

Throw snowballs!"

But

Shirley and Sammy,

and

Robert and Richie,

and

Frances and Sandy

would not move at all.

They did not even blink.

"I give up!"

cried Mr. Green.

He dragged himself into the house,

where Mrs. Green warmed him up

with cabbage soup.

A week before Christmas,

Mr. Green still had no picture

of his family.

He sat in the kitchen with Mrs. Green

looking at all the terrible pictures.

Shirley and Sammy came in for cookies.

They looked at the spring picture

of Shirley pinching Sammy.

"That was dopey!" Sammy said.

"It was fun," said Shirley.

Shirley tickled him.

Sammy giggled.

Robert and Richie

looked at the summer picture

of the snake hissing at the frog

and giggled even louder.

Frances and Sandy ran in

to put snowballs in the freezer.

They laughed

at the autumn picture

of everyone jumping

off the apple tree.

Shirley and Sammy,

and

Robert and Richie,

and

Frances and Sandy

laughed their heads off.

Suddenly they heard

CLICK!

57

"GOT YOU!" bellowed Mr. Green.

"I just got the most perfect

happy Christmas picture."

"Hooray!" everyone shouted.

"Double hooray," said Mrs. Green.

On Christmas day,

Mr. Green put

the perfect Christmas picture

in the middle

of the holiday table.

"What a joyful family we have,"

he told Mrs. Green.

"Indeed we do!" she said.

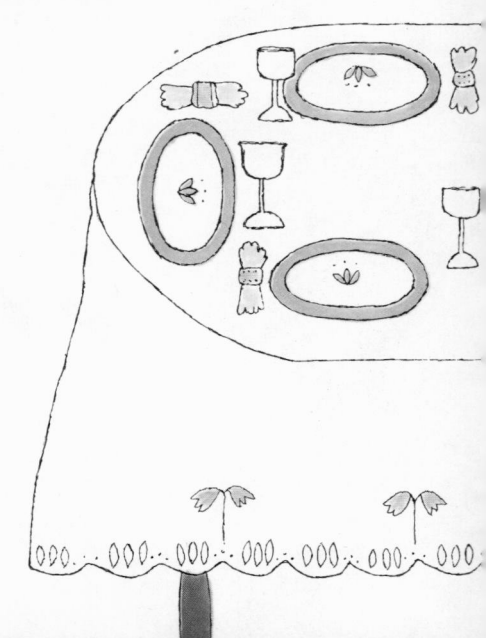

And they all sat down

to a huge Christmas dinner.

Merry Christmas